**More titles from Finding My Way Books**

*Kaitlyn Wants To See Ducks*
*I Don't Know If I Want a Puppy*
*Marco and I Want To Play Ball*
*MyaGrace Wants To Make Music*
*Reese Has a Halloween Secret*

Copyright © 2015 Finding My Way Books
All rights reserved.
ISBN: 978-0-9903543-2-1

# I Want To Be Like Poppin' Joe

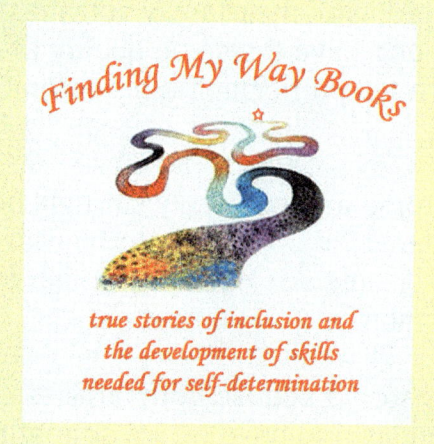

*Finding My Way Books*

true stories of inclusion and
the development of skills
needed for self-determination

By Jo Meserve Mach and
Vera Lynne Stroup-Rentier

Photography by Mary Birdsell

Our reason for sharing this story…

Joe is an adult with Down Syndrome and Autism. He is leading a self-determined life. His parents advocated for him to participate in meaningful inclusive experiences throughout his childhood. He liked to be busy so he helped with housework, took swimming lessons, and participated in all their family activities. They believed that he could grow up and have the same quality of life as his older siblings. Today Joe is a full participant in his community as a businessman.

Dylan has Down Syndrome and his family strongly believes in including him in their family life. He loves to be with his brother, playing with their dog or outside. He loves to help dad in the yard. He loves to cook with mom.

We chose to write this story because both families demonstrate how to follow a child's interests and build on his strengths. This, in turn, promotes the skills needed for self-determination. Joe is a full participant in his family and community through his business.

We are happy to share their stories.
~Jo, Vera and Mary

*A True Story Promoting
Inclusion and Self-Determination*

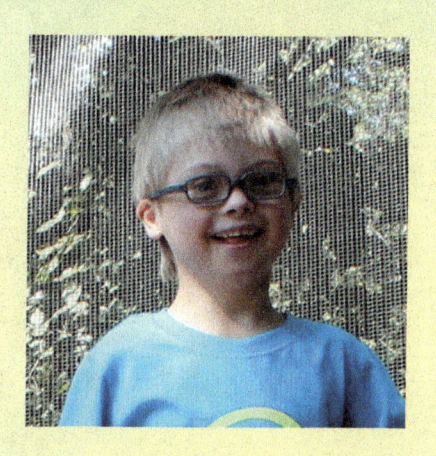

Finding My Way Books is dedicated to celebrating the success of inclusion by sharing stories about children with special needs in families and communities.

For more information:
www.findingmywaybooks.com

I'm Dylan and this is Poppin' Joe.
He's my friend.

1

He likes to clean cars. He likes to fill cups.
He likes to be with his dad.
He likes to juggle. He likes to be busy.

He had to decide what he liked best.
He picked making popcorn with his dad.
It keeps him busy. Now that's his job.

I like to play with my dog. I like to give hugs.
I like to be with my dad. I like to dig.
I like to be outside.

Poppin' Joe learned how to make popcorn.
He knows how to mix corn, sugar, and oil.
He knows just the right parts.

This is what I like to mix.
I can be like Poppin' Joe.

Poppin' Joe weighs sugar.
He knows how much to use.

I can weigh plants.
I can be like Poppin' Joe.

Poppin' Joe knows how to listen.
Pop, pop, pop, pop..pop...pop....pop.
He knows when the popcorn is done.

I listen to Dad. He tells me how to plant.
I can be like Poppin' Joe.

Poppin' Joe knows how much salt to use.
He counts the shakes of salt it needs.

I can count plants. I count 1, 2, 3.
I can be like Poppin' Joe.

Poppin' Joe knows when to dump popcorn.

I can dump dirt.
I can be like Poppin' Joe.

Poppin' Joe knows how to rake popcorn.
He helps it cool down.

I can rake.
I can be like Poppin' Joe.

Poppin' Joe knows how to shovel popcorn.
He puts it in bags to sell.

I can shovel dirt.
I can be like Poppin' Joe.

Poppin' Joe knows how to load popcorn.

I can load plants.
I can be like Poppin' Joe.

Poppin' Joe knows how to sell his popcorn.
He gets money.

I get money for working in the yard.
I can be like Poppin' Joe.

Poppin' Joe knows how to work hard.

23

I work hard helping my dad.
I can be like Poppin' Joe.

Poppin' Joe likes what he decided to do.
He's the boss.

Someday, I'll decide what I like to do best.

Someday, I'm going to be the boss.
I want to be like Poppin' Joe.

*Thank you to Dylan's and Joe's families
for sharing their stories.*

## 'I Want To Be Like Poppin' Joe' Index

Skills promoting self- determination are seen in this book:
    Page 2 and page 4- cultivate your child's interests
    Pages 5-24- build on your child's strengths
    Page 3- encourage choice making

Pg. 32 Information about Self-Determination

Pg. 33-34 Family Guide for promoting Self-Determination

Pg. 36 Classroom Activities

Pg. 38 Finding My Way Books' Team

Pg. 40 Contact Finding My Way Books

Pg. 42 Contact Poppin' Joe

# Encouraging self-determination skill building in children

Our books are written in the actual voice of a child. The child is telling their story of how they are learning to be more self- determined

Here are examples of self-determination skills:
1. Choice making
2. Decision making
3. Problem solving
4. Goal setting and planning
5. Self-direction behaviors (self-regulation)
6. Responsibility
7. Independence
8. Self-awareness and self-knowledge
9. Self-advocacy and leadership
10. Communication
11. Participation
12. Having relationships and social connections

Weir, K., Cooney, M., Walter, M., Moss, C., & Carter, E. W. (2011). Fostering self-determination among children with disabilities: Ideas from parents for parents. *Madison, WI: Natural Supports Project, Waisman Center, University of Wisconsin—Madison.*

# Family Guide for Promoting Self-Determination

**Cultivate your child's interests:**

This story shares many of Joe's and Dylan's interests. Joe's parents followed his interests as they expolred a variety of volunteer and job opportunities for Joe. These included vacuuming at the church, doing yard work, and being part of the maintenance crew for a community swimming pool.
Dylan's parents provide Dylan with many opportunities to be outside. He works with Dad, plays with his brother, Jacob, and plays with the family dog. He also likes to help his Mom when she bakes.

**Build on your child's strengths:**

Joe's strengths include being a hard worker, pleasing people by doing what he is asked to do, liking order or neatness, laughing and having a good time. It was important to Joe's parents that his job build on all these strengths. The Kettle Korn business requires him to work hard, keep the booth organized and neat, to be with many people, and allows him to have a good time with his family and co-workers.
Dylan has wonderful strengths. He loves to laugh and tease people. He is a great hugger. He is good at convincing others to do things by telling them to "try it" or "do it" or by asking "please." Dylan's strengths help him succeed at school.

**Encourage your child to make choices and participate in decision making:**

Joe chose his haircut. He wanted a 'Joe-hawk' cut. Joe chooses which task he wants to do in the Kettle Korn process. He is the boss. All the employees know that when Joe wants to change and do a different task, that is his right, and they are to shift what they are doing to support this. Learning to make choices builds toward the ability to make decisions. Joe was able to participate in the decision to work in the Kettle Korn business.
Choices can be offered with any activity. For example, Dylan's Dad can ask Dylan which plant he wants to dig up.

**Have the expectation that your child can get a job and be an active member of his or her community as an adult:**

At Joe's final IEP meeting, his parents were told he would work in a sheltered workshop and live in a group home. But at his birth, Joe's parents consciously made a promise to give him a quality life equal to that of his siblings. This meant he would be a part of his community and to have friends.
Dylan's parents are already thinking about Dylan's future job. They also want him to be an active member of his community. We'll have to wait and see where Dylan's enthusiasm takes him.

35

# Classroom Activities for I Want To Be Like Poppin' Joe

1. Strengths and interests:
Have each student draw or write down their three interests and three strengths. In the story Joe shows his interests include juggling, being busy, cleaning cars, filling cups and being with his Dad. Joe's strengths include knowing how to listen, knowing how to load things and being able to measure things correctly.

2. Discovering a job you'd like to do:
Have each student think about a job that matches his or her interests and strengths. In the story Dylan thinks about his interests that include being outside with his dad, digging, being with his dog and giving hugs. Dylan's strengths include enjoying being around others, physically being able to work in the yard with his dad, and following directions. Dylan shows in the book that he could someday work with plants for his job.

3. Sharing:
Have each student share what they think they'd like to do for a job someday and how that choice is based on their interests and strengths.

**Finding My Way Books**

*true stories of inclusion and the development of skills needed for self-determination*

Jo Meserve Mach spent 36 years as an Occupational Therapist. She is very passionate about inclusion and the development of skills needed for self-determination and independence. Jo views inclusion from a functional perspective. She hopes our books share how children with special needs can be actively involved in their daily lives. Increasing the participation and engagement of children and young adults with disabilities into family and community activities, enriches the lives of everyone. She believes all children have incredible strengths that sometimes just need some environmental adaptations to help them be realized.

Vera Lynne Stroup-Rentier has 25 years of experience teaching within the fields of Early Childhood and Special Education. She has a PhD in Special Education from the University of Kansas. Her current work as the Assistant Director on the state Early Childhood, Special Education, and Title Services team at the Kansas State Department of Education gives her the opportunity to shape policy decisions impacting the lives of students with special educational needs. Vera is passionate about the inclusion of each and every child in settings where they would be if they did not have a disability. She brings the perspective of inclusion and the promotion of self-determination from her work with families, teachers and therapists over her 25 year career. Parenting a teen and tween with special needs enrich her life.

Mary Birdsell is a freelance photographer and a former middle school Speech and Theatre teacher. She brings her talents in art and design to our books. Mary strives to create images that reflect the strengths of each child. She feels that an image can project a child's voice and abilities within their environment. Mary's background in education, theatre and photography intersect as she visually creates our books. Within each story, she uses colors and shapes to promote the child's growth and development of skills needed for self-determination as demonstrated through their story.

MyaGrace Rentier is a middle school student. She loves music and has a gift for enthusiasm. MyaGrace demonstrated her self-advocacy skills by telling her mother that she would like to talk about books to help our team. Today she shares her gift of enthusiasm by helping promote all our 'Finding My Way' books.

For more information about all of our titles and to purchase books: www.findingmywaybooks.com

Contact us at:
findingmywaybooks@gmail.com

*For more information about Poppin' Joe's Gourmet Kettle Korn:*
*www.poppinjoes.com*

CPSIA information can be obtained
at www.ICGtesting.com
Printed in the USA
LVOW02s1618210816
501267LV00017B/430/P